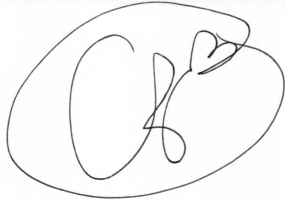

Chapter One:

On the Move

Alabama has changed. It has changed BIG TIME. Since Mo Lemont has moved from New York City, it has been different. Let me tell you the story about the girl who could sing.

Mo realized that New York isn't the best place to express her feelings in song. Let's just say people aren't the nicest in that city. If she went down the sidewalk humming, no one would notice. She tried humming louder, but then people plugged their ears.

Her mother, Georgia Lemont, was a saleswoman that needed a new job. Just like Mo, no one wanted to hear it. Commercials, knocking on doors, business cards! It just didn't work out.

The two had enough money to move, and they wanted a home just right for them.

They checked, and the closest family that they could move in with lived in Alabama!

The flight was very long in Mo's opinion, but the car ride from the airport to their family's house was only 45 minutes. They were moving in with Mo's Aunt Nina and Uncle Jared. Mo opened their door. "Hey guys!"

"Mo, Georgia!" Nina exclaimed.

They all hugged, when *someone* came into the room.

It was Racheal, Mo's cousin, Georgia's niece, Jared and Nina's daughter. The brattiest in the family. The darkness of the house. The nightmare of the goldfish. The bully of the school. The queen of the texting. The cousin of the Mo. Yep, that's Racheal.

Racheal had always been jealous of Mo's singing talent, and how she always had perfect hair without trying. She hated how she was always nice and had perfect grades. That caused her to be incredibly mean to her.

She was also bratty to other people because she just to fit in and be liked. Mo being perfect and moving in didn't help that subject.

"Oh! Racheal!" Mo said flatly. She had almost forgot. Maybe this move wasn't as great as she thought it would be.

"Just because you're moving in, doesn't mean we're going to be friends," she replied, not looking up from her phone. Her accent wasn't as strong as her parents', but her makeup sure was.

"Oh, okay," Mo answered softly.

"Racheal South!" Aunt Nina shouted. "You do NOT

talk to your cousin like that!" She turned to Mo. "I apologize. And I know Racheal *won't*."

"Whatever," the brat scoffed. She walked in the other room.

"I'll go talk to her," suggested Uncle Jared reluctantly.

"You go do that," Nina agreed. "I'll go show these two their rooms."

Mo nodded her head vigorously.

Fortunately, Mo wasn't

cursed with the "privilege" of sleeping in the same room with her...*dear* cousin. Although, Racheal's room *was* next door.

Georgia got to sleep next to her sister and brother-in-law's room DOWNSTAIRS. Mo and Racheal were UPSTAIRS. ALONE.

"This can't end well," Mo thought. "If it even DOES end."

Chapter Two: Racheal and Music

It was the awkwardest dinner EVER. Racheal was texting with her left hand and eating with her right. Jared's eating was loud, and you could really hear it over the silence. No one knew what to say. Even Aunt Nina.

"So..." Georgia suggested, "how about you tell the children about the," she cleared her throat, "banquet tomorrow." She was looking at

Nina who wasblankly staring into her spaghetti. Georgia cleared her throat as loud as she could.

That startled her sister.

"Oh!" Nina jumped. THAT startled Racheal. Mo giggled. When everyone stared at her, she recovered it with a fake cough.

"The BANQUET," Georgia reminded Nina.

"Oh!" she realized. That seemed to be the only word she said so far.

"What banquet?" Mo asked, trying to be part of the conversation. She sprinkled some parmesan cheese on her dinner after pouring loads of tomato sauce on. "Yes, the pizza banquet," Nina remembered, sighing. "Celebrating the 15th anniversary of Mobile Pizzeria."

"Ugh, we have to go *this* year, too?" Racheal whined, rolling her eyes.

"Yes, honey, just like we've gone every year since you were five," Jared answered.

"I'm thirteen!" she shouted, finally looking up from her phone.

"And I'm forty-six!" he replied. "I'm twelve!" Mo blurted.

"I'm Nina! Nice to meet you all!" Nina exclaimed jokingly.

Dinner ended on a giggle. Well, everyone except *Racheal*. While she left to go to her room (the first time she wasn't *told* to), the rest of the family actually *cleared* their dishes. Mo went to pick up Racheal's plate when Nina refused, "I got it sweetie."

"Okay, Aunt Nina," she replied. You can't argue with your aunt.

It was soon nine, time to go to sleep. Mo got her pajamas on and brushed her teeth. She got in bed and fell asleep.

"Wow, your daughter follows directions *so* WELL!" Nina exclaimed to Georgia. She took a sip of her tea. "Racheal ends up sleeping in her clothes, like her dress or something." "Yeah, Mo seems to be more into singing than fashion," Georgia explained. She laughed. "She even hums in her sleep!"

"Yeah," said Nina, looking at the ground.

After a second or two, her eyes began to widen, and her face took on a worried look. "Did you say...HUM?!"

Georgia nodded in reply.

As the moms were talking, the girls did what they usually did at nine. Racheal texting on her phone in her bed and Mo sleeping. Speaking of Mo sleeping, I'm *sure* you heard the mom's conversation. Mo HUMS in her sleep as you heard. I bet you didn't know Racheal HATES music. Unusual, right? She's more of a texter. Nina assumed if Racheal heard Mo's humming next door, she'd flip. Her assumption was correct. Unfortunately.

Mo was just humming a nice *Twinkle Twinkle* when Racheal heard. She plugged her ears. That seemed to work, until Mo started to hum some rock music. Racheal covered her *delicate* ears with a pillow. It still didn't work! She was starting to get REALLY frustrated. So, Racheal decided to stop it. She got out of her bed and put her phone down (which is rare). She stomped out of her room and into Mo's.

Racheal hated music, but she had to admit Mo's singing was...decent.

She snapped herself out of nonsense and went to wake her cousin up. She hesitated.

"Should I *really* do this?" she thought, when she heard

her mother and aunt whispering up the stairs. "Oh, no, I have to hide!"

So, she hid in the closet. She was starting to get used to the humming.

"To be honest, she's not bad," Racheal thought. She was as silent as a mouse that was asked to be quiet to get a piece of cheese.

"Where's Racheal?" she heard Georgia's ruffled voice say.

"Probably off doing some mischief hold on..." Nina

replied.

"What?" Georgia asked, worriedly.

"Check Mo's room," Nina answered calmly, but her expression was not ascalm as her voice.

Georgia obeyed her sister, and to Racheal's surprise, the closet was the first place her aunt Georgia looked...

Chapter Three: Racheal's Freedom

Racheal tried to push herself to the left when Georgia looked to the right, but then she suddenly remembered: the guest room (now Mo's room) closet was only 5 feet wide! She tiptoed backwards and hid herself in all of Mo's dresses and casual shirts. She covered herself just in the nick of time. Getting rid of the humming wasn't so important, just not getting in trouble.

You may be wondering why it was *so* important not to get in trouble. Her phone is the answer. Nina said that the next time she got in trouble (which would be this time if she got caught) she would take away her phone for a whole *day*. A DAY! That was a *huge* deal for Racheal, and she did NOT want that to happen.

Georgia opened the closet and looked around. LOOKED. Not searched! So, she found nothing.

"Nothing here," she muttered to herself.

"Yes!" Racheal mouthed. She couldn't make a movement *or* a peep. Racheal was grateful for mouthing.

When the coast was clear, and Racheal heard nothing but a quiet hum, she silently and I mean SILENTLY crept out of Mo's room and into hers. She jumped onto her bed and set up the act that made it look like she was asleep the whole night. No that was too obvious she hid under her covers and pretended to text her friends. Nope, she didn't have to pretend. Racheal texted her thumbs off until she eventually fell asleep.

Meanwhile, Mo was dreaming. Mo was dreaming *hard*. She was thinking about her future (Which wasn't very important at twelve, but she was). Her what seemed to be great future. She was singing on the stage, when the song record came to a blazing screech. Racheal stepped on the stage and shouted, "No go for Mo!" Then she started a chant saying those exact words.

Mo stopped humming in her sleep and woke up from a terrifying nightmare. She looked out the window behind her and glanced at the clock. It looked five-ish out the window and it was six-ish on the clock. Mo decided to sleep in a little more.

The thing about Racheal is that she goes to sleep *and* wakes up REALLY late. So, she didn't wake up until 11:00. Mo ended up getting downstairs for breakfast at 8:00. Breakfast was cornflakes, just like every Monday morning (by the way, if you didn't know, it's summer for Mo and Racheal).

"Ugh, cornflakes*again*?" askedRacheal, checking her social media. "I'm going to the store today before the banquet," Aunt Nina assured her. "Right now, cornflakes are your only option. Well, unless you want fruit."

"Cornflakes are good!" Racheal replied quickly.

"Where are the bowls?" Mo questioned.

"I'll get you one, hon," Uncle

Jared answered. "For next time, though, they're in the left cabinet on the right side of the kitchen."

"Are you guys excited for the" Georgia started to say.

Aunt Nina covered her sister's mouth and interrupted, "the great day we are going to have!" Mo raised a brow, confused.

"Don't remind her," whispered Nina to Georgia.

Georgia nodded, knowingly.

"Yeah, the pizza banquet's

gonna be the best!" Uncle Jared exclaimed.

Nina looked at her husband with an annoying look.

"What?" he asked, cluelessly.

"Ugh, we have to? that stupid thing," Racheal remembered, groaning. "Do *I* have to?"

"That's what," Nina replied to Jared. She looked at Racheal. "Yes, you do." "Come on, it'll be fun!" Georgia said to her niece.

Mo would have said exactly whather mom had said if she had the guts to.

"It wasn't fun the last eight years,"

Racheal muttered.

"Maybe since Mo is gonna be there, it will be okay," Nina suggested, shrugging.

"Yeah, right," she scoffed.

Nina suddenly had an idea. "Okay, fine, you don't have to go to the banquet. After all your begging, what else can I do?"

"Are you SERIOUS?" Racheal asked,

surprised. "YES!"

Mo, Georgia, and Jared were confused.

I'll explain later," Nina told the three.

Racheal heard what she said, but she wasn't listening. She was busy texting her friends that she was FREE!!! She had no idea her mom had a plan...and a *really* good one it was.

Chapter Four:
The Pizza Banquet Trick

"That'll keep her quiet," Georgia said to Nina after she explained her sinister plan.

"Yeah, but isn't she going to be suspicious when you tell her we're going to the grocery store?" Mo asked. "How are you going to get her to get in the car with us a half hour before the banquet?"

"Trust me, she's always *so* distracted with her phone,

she doesn't care where we're going," Nina explained, she knew *a lot* about Racheal. "This is a *very* brutal and mischievous plan, Nina!" Georgia said to her sister. "I like it!"

Mo giggled. She had never heard her mom say something like that. Something so dark, evil, and childish...She loved it!

The five people in the house were greatly anticipating that afternoon. Mo was excited for her first Mobile Pizza banquet.

Georgia was excited for her sister's plan to succeed. Nina was excited to have fun with her prospering family. Racheal was excited to have her freedom from family and pizza. Jared was just excited to eat pizza, period.

While the five were waiting to go to the

grocery store, they all did their own thing. Mo practiced her amazical singing. Georgia was looking in the newspaper to see if they had any jobs open in Mobile, Alabama. Nina was reserving a table at

Mobile Pizzeria for later that day. Racheal was picking out her outfit for her freedom night! Jared was looking on the Mobile pizza menu to choose his toppings (Nina suggested that because he can never decide what to eat under the pressuring ten minutes he usually had).

When it was finally time, everyone got ready to go to the grocery store, and what Racheal didn't know: the pizza banquet.

"Racheal, honey, we have to go to the grocery store!" Nina

shouted upstairs from down. "Come on, let's go!"

"Wait, I thought you said I wasn't going to the banquet," Racheal replied, stomping down the stairs.

"I need you to come to...uh, point out which ice cream you want for tonight," her mother replied. "Yep, that's it."

"Ugh," Racheal groaned. "Fine."

She was fine with this, as long as she didn't need to go to that banquet. She realized her mom gave up making her go, so why not give her a break?

"Let's go!" Mo exclaimed with pep in her step. "This is gonna be fun!"

"Why are you so excited to go to the grocery store?" Racheal questioned.

"Um...erg, they, uh..." Mo stuttered. "They have...yummy cookie taste testing!"

"Oh, yay!" Racheal answered sarcastically. "This is the best day ever! What if it's one with sprinkles? Ooh!!!"

Mo gave her cousin a *real mature Racheal* look.

They all got their shoes on and went out in the summer sun.

The ride to the store was interesting.

The radio was going haywire. Every time Racheal's mom turned on the radio, she put on her headphones and listened to the wonderful sound of texting ringtones.

Mo was looking out the window, trying to plug her ears. She was humming to herself to try to distract her mind and ears from the car's noise.

Jared was talking to Georgia about the time he went fishing with his best friend. That was a crazy day with Gerald! Of course, Georgia was laughing reacting to the hilarious memories her brother-in-law had in Alabama.

Nina was focusing on the road, trying to sing what the radio had provided her. That didn't really work out, unless the new hip song's only lyric was "SCREECH!SCREECH!"

To the grocery store was fifteen minutes,

not including the time it took to park. For goodness sake, it took them five whole minutes to find out a place for the car to stay! Apparently, a LOT of moms in Mobile, Alabama shopped on Mondays for food.

The Lemonts needed to get to that banquet! And fast!

The five got out of their car and ran/walked/slumped/skipp

edintothestore.I bet you can guess who did which.

"Hello, welcome to Munchie Mandy's," a man in red welcomed them. "Feel free to grab some cookie samples at the back of the store."

"Your favorite," Racheal whispered to Mo.

"Uh, yay!" Mo exclaimed, trying as hard as she could to sound believable.

"Whatever," her cousin replied, rolling her eyes.

"Thank you, sir," Nina said

to the man while Mo and Racheal were whispering. "Come on, guys, we gotta go!"

"What's the rush?" Racheal groaned. "I can't run in these heels!"

"We need to...get to the cookie samples before they run out!" Georgia explained: she didn't sound as believable as Mo because she did NOT have a good poker face when she fibbed.

"What is it with you and your cookie samples?" Racheal asked as they walked into the huge building.

"We need to get dish soap, pancakes, and ice cream," Jared told everybody, looking at the list. "Not a lot of things."

His stomach rumbled.

"Pancakes are over there!" Nina exclaimed, she practically knew the whole store by heart.

Mo followed behind everyone, realizing her aunt was the alpha in the grocery store situation. She recognized the store, but she didn't know where everything was.

She barely even went to her own grocery store, there would be a chance she could get lost in a place she lived almost right next to!

Soon they were in the *Cold Delightful Treats* aisle, or at least that's what the sign said. They had already got the dish soap and pancakes, now they needed one more thing: the ice cream.

Racheal ran to the ice cream, still staring at her

phone (it was the only thing besides make up, fashion, and texting/social media that interested her).

"Careful, you might hurt yourself,"Nina suggested. "Plus, how are you going to pick out your ice cream when you're looking at your"

"Got it," Racheal interrupted. She held her second favorite ice cream in her hand and plopped it in the cart, for she had just finished a carton of her first favorite.

"Never mind," Nina said.

"Okay, let's go!" Jared exclaimed impatiently. "I'm hungry!"

"Of course you are," his daughter scoffed. "Since when have you not been?"

Mo gave him the same *real mature, Racheal* look she gave her cousin, except she meant it to be a *how foolish, Uncle Jared!*

They all rushed out of the store as fast as they could. Racheal had no idea why they were running out of a grocery store with worried faces. She assumed her father was hangry and nobody wanted to see his crankiness.

They all buckled up and headed off to the banquet. Racheal didn't know the trail had been different from the one they used to use for going to the house because she never paid attention to the road. She was always paying attention to her phone.

When they arrived at their destination, Racheal looked up from her phone. "Oh, no."

Chapter Five
Spotlight on Mo

"Please tell me we're taking abathroom break," Racheal said to her family.

"Nope, we tricked you!" Georgia exclaimed, satisfied with her *amazing* acting skills.

"Ugh, NOOOOOOOT COOOOOOOOOOOOL!" Racheal whined.

"Come on, let's go in!" Jared squirmed, anxious to get his hands on some chicken, anchovy, pepperoni pizza (he decided to go simple)

"Fine!" Racheal screamed, attracting attention. "There's no way out anyway. I can't walk home because of these heels. Well, actually, I wouldn't walk home ever, even in designer sneakers."

The five all went in the pizzeria, Nina in front and Racheal in back. There weren't many people in the restaurant, but just enough for a banquet.

"Welcome, welcome!" a woman behind a desk greeted

everybody.

Mo looked at the menu above the lady.

Wow, there were a *lot* of choices! She was starting to understand why her uncle took hours to decide.

They went up to the desk and ordered their meals. Coincidentally (not really), the five all ordered pizza. They could have ordered pasta, or chicken fingers. I guess they were just in the mood for pizza.

They patiently waited at

their table for entertainment to start. It was takingan awfully long time. Mo was starting to think the waiting would *never* end!

Suddenly, Racheal noticed something. Or should I say...someONE? Her heart pumped like it never did before. She set down her phone for the SECOND time THIS WEEK!!! Mo and Georgia moving in had changed her. Anyway, she couldn't set her eyes off a dreamy boy whom she had instantly fell in like with, . her feet carried her over to him, Racheal's eyes fluttering like how a butterfly flapped its colorful, symmetrical, wings.

"Hey," the boy said. "What's up?" "Hehe," Racheal croaked dreamily.

"My name's Michael," he replied. Heheld out his hand for a shake. "What's yours?" "R--Racheal," she answered. "So..." "So..." he said back.

Racheal opened her mouth to speak when the same woman that greeted her interrupted: "There is a *little* change in plans."

The audience of what would be a show looked confused and surprised.

"The band that was supposed to come and perform tonight..." the woman hesitated, not wanting to let the customers down, "...couldn't make it..."

Some people *aww*-ed, some booed, but the audience was still understanding.

A man whispered something in her ear.

She nodded, excitedly. This was a new thing for her.

"There is a way to solve the problem, though," the woman announced, causing the people's frowns to fade away. "Do we have any singers in here that would be willing to perform for us?"

No one raised their hand except for this woman in black that had a very serious look on her face be here an hour ago."

"So, they're not coming?" theserious woman asked. "I'm

their agent, and they said they would

"I'm sorry ma'am, they called us and said they couldn't make it here," the woman that spoke the news explained.

"They would have told me," the agentreplied. Suddenly a sound of a texting ringtone loudly rang, echoing in the room. Racheal immediately stopped staring at Michael and checked her phone. The agent checked hers, too. "Okay, *now* they tell me."

"Anyways,"thewoman

shouted. "Anyone?"

Nina nudged Mo.

"What?" Mo asked, a little alarmed. "What is it?"

"You can sing, honey!" Nina answered encouragingly. "Raise your hand!"

Georgia overheard their talking. "Nina, I don't know," she whispered. "I--"

"We're doing this," her sister interrupted.

She grabbed her niece's arm and forced it to raise in the air, as if she were volunteering.

"Ding, ding, we have a winner!" the woman told everybody, pointing to Mo.

"What?" Racheal muttered madly.

"What?" Mo muttered madly. She could sing, but in front of everybody? What song would she sing? What instrument would she use? What would everyone think of her? These questions whirled around in her head like leaves on a windy day. Her heart beat more than

Racheal's did when she got a new phone. The fifth time. Not the fourth, not the sixth, but the fifth. That time just seemed more special than any of the others. Back to the story now.

Mo slowly walked up to the microphone the speaker was using. She glanced at the agent who was curious to see if Mo could really sing. When she looked at Mo the girl looked away, pretending she didn't see anything.

"Um...hi, my name is Mo Lemont," she announced to

everyone nervously. "So... I guess I could sing a song that I wrote myself."

The woman who had the microphone asked Mo if she could tell the audience something real quick before she sang. "We unfortunately have no instruments, uh, Miss Lemont can use, so, can we all clap to the beat?

The audience cheered with agreement.

Well, everyone except RACHEAL. Of course, the grump didn't like music, but to make it worse, her *annoying* cousin Mo was singing.

Mo started to sing weakly, but as she got more comfortable with the audience, she was more confident and loud. They cheered, and they clapped while Racheal groaned, and she stomped.

When she was done with the AMAZING song, the audience cheered even louder than when she was singing: not wanting to be rude.

"Ugh, that was terrible,

wasn't it?" Racheal asked Michael, nudging him with her elbow. "What an amateur."

"*I* actually thought she was pretty good," he disagreed. "I mean, she wrote that song herself..."

"She's my cousin, and honestly, she's done better," Racheal explained. Her jealousy was growing as they spoke! "I don't think she's a good singer."

"Well I DO," he said, taking Mo's side, "I respect your opinion, but that's kind of rude. Especially to your cousin."

Michael walked away from what seemed to him a terrible person.

"*Great,*" Racheal muttered. "I lost him...now back to the phone!"

Mo walked back over to her mother and aunt.

"Great job, Mo!" Nina exclaimed. "That was amazing!" Georgia agreed.

"Excuse me, Mo Lemont?" the agent said

to Mo, tapping her shoulder. "Can I talk to you for asecond?"

"Sure, what is it?" she answered, a bit nervously.

"I was wondering if you would like to join my recording studio, you know, as an artist," the agent explained.

"OMG!!!" Mo was thinking. "This is such an honor, this is the best day of mylife!"

Although, what she thought was *very* different from what she SAID.

"Let me ask my mother," Mo replied, "thank you very much."

"Mom can I--" she started to say.

"I heard the conversation," Georgia interrupted. There was a pause. "Of course you can, honey! This is a once in a lifetime opportunity!"

"Oh my gosh, thank you *so* much!" Mo exclaimed with so much gratitude.

She walked over to the agent and told her the great news.

"That's amazing news!" she replied. "I'm just going to need you to sign a couple of contracts."

"Okay," croaked Mo.

The agent took a stack of papers out of her purse and handed them to Mo. She took on a worried look when Mo saw the many papers handed onto her.

"Just get these done by tomorrow, and we'll keep in touch," the agent explained, handing her business card. "Justemail me when you've finished; around five o'clock P.M. would be good."

"Um, I, uh...okay," Mo answered hesitantly.

She walked over to her mother again and handed her the contracts. Georgia's eyes widened when she saw that the stack was three inches tall!

"Honey, what are these?" she asked her daughter.

"Contracts," Mo answered. "And a *lot* of em'."

"When are you supposed to

get these done?" Georgia questioned.

"YoumeanWE?"Moreplied. "These have to be done TOMORROW."

"Maybe we can make an extension,"Nina suggested.

"Good idea," said Mo, turning around.

She saw no agent. She looked around and didn't see her. She probably left! "Maybe I can email her."

She put her hand in her pocket and found no business

card. She started to panic when she found nothing in the other one. "Oh, no! What am I gonna *do*?!"

Mo's head was racing like a race car speeding on a track. She HAD to find that business card. And quick!

Chapter Six:
The Lost Card

Only a dog could have found that business card. Humans don't have the sense of smell they do. Mo had no idea where that business card was, and she had a feeling she wouldn't find it in time. The banquet was over, and the pizzeria was closing in ten minutes. What if she had to fill out all those contracts? She needed all the help she could get.

Everyone was looking everywhere, employees moving objects and customers looking in corners for the card.

Mo was running all around the restaurant, nervously looking for it.

Suddenly, an employee shouted, "I found a business card!"

Mo ran over to him, clawing the card out of his hand. Her face fell when she saw a bright pink business card with a cupcake on it dangling from her hands.

"This isn't the one I'm looking for, this one is for 'Abby's Bakery'," Mo told him, disappointed.

She slumped over to Georgia. "Found anything?"

"Nope," her mother replied. "Sorry, honey."

"I can't do all of those contracts!" she sighed.

"I'll help you," Georgia suggested, "and so will your aunt Nina."

"Even with TEN people we

couldn't get those done!" Mo exclaimed. "What do we do?"

"Hmm..." Georgia thought. "What *can* we do?"

"I've got it!" Nina suddenly shouted. "I've got a plan!"

"Another one?" Racheal asked, walking over to the three ladies.

"Ooh, yay!" Georgia added. "Another one!"

Mo smirked at the thought her aunt had a plan and that her mom had that childish look on her face again.

"What is it?" Mo immediately questioned impatiently. "What's the plan?"

"Okay, here it is: I say we go to that music store downtown," Nina suggested. "Someone OUGHT to know the agency."

"Well, not as mischievous as I was imagining, but I have no arguments," Georgia replied. "You're the professional planner here."

"It sounds like the only option we have," Mo added,

shrugging.

"Ugh, fine," Racheal interrupted.

They told everyone they would stop everyone they would stop looking in the pizzeria but in the music store. So, they all exited the building, even the employees! I guess the banquet was the only part of the day the restaurant was open.

As the Lemonts were heading out, Michael sneaked a wink at Mo. Her cheeks turned red, and whenever she thought about it that day, she blushed.

The music store was a small, purplebuilding with a sign that read *Muzic*. Apparently, any word with an *S* turned automatically cool if you slapped a *Z* in its place.

They walked inside and saw headphones and music CDs hung up everywhere.

There was a teenager behind a desk, smacking gum and redoing her eyeshadow. If you asked her, you could probably find a lot of things that she had in common with Racheal.

"Um, excuse me," Nina asked the teen. "Do you know any agents nearby, specifically ones with business cards?"

"No ma'am," she replied in an Alabama accent, staring at her phone.

Coincidentally, so was Racheal.

Mo looked from the employee to Racheal and smirked. They could be good friends if they tried.

Racheal turned up her sound effects so you could hear them from her earbuds from one foot away, trying to block out what they were saying. She wasn't *trying* to get the gum smacker's attention.

She looked up at Racheal. "What kind of phone do you have?"

"Megatro eight," Racheal answered.

"Megatro NINE," the employee bragged.

Racheal looked up. She took a piece of paper out of her

pocket and gave it to her new texting buddy. It was her email.

"Text me," she told her.

"I might know where the agent is," the teen said, grabbing the paper out of her hand. "There's a music studio aboutfive buildings away from her labeled *Rock Studioz* with a *Z*."

Mo smiled. Her cousin made a friend (or a "texter") and they might find the agent! She was getting more confident, until her mother dragged her down.

"I hope she's not sending us on a wild goose chase," she said to her daughter. She looked at Racheal then back to Mo. "You know how teens can be these days."

"Have hope," Jared suggested, "we will probably find the agent."

"Thanks, Uncle J," Mo thanked. That really lifted her spirit.

They all walked out of the store, Racheal smiling to herself. It always feels good to make a new friend, or as Racheal calls it, a "texter".

Mo automatically saw the bright blue sign that was labeled "Rock Studioz". Again with the "z" thing!

"You have such good eyes," Nina commented as her niece ran to the studio. She was impatient, had a competitive uncle, and had a lot of energy. Mix those three together and you get Jared racing Mo to the building.

Nina and Georgia did the "Mom run" where it's sort of

like fast walking. Itwas like what second graders do when the teachers tell them not to run but they're still super impatient.

On the other hand, Racheal walked behind them all, staring at her phone. Mo slowed down when she got to the door, for if she busted in a big studio unexpectedly, bad things could happen. She could disturb the artists and get kicked out! That would lead to doing all those contracts. Ugh!

She silently opened the

door knob and made sure her mom was right behind her. Right when they walked in the building, they realized it seemed bigger on the inside than on the outside.

"Hello, how may I help you?" a woman asked behind a dark brown desk.

"May we please see if you have any agents in the building?" Mo asked all angel-like.

"Okay, here's the thing: you may search for an agent upstairs, but you may *not* under *any* circumstances disturb the artists," the lady explained firmly. "I'm not sure an agent is here right now; the attendance sheet was taken to the printer to be copied."

"Okay," Nina agreed, leading the pack up the long staircase.

They saw a long hallway that lead to a right turn that had another hallway attached to it. The hallway had doors on each side, covering the building with rooms.

"How are we going to find the agent if we 'can't disturb

the artists'?" Mo asked, discouraged. "There are a *million* rooms in here!"

"Calm down," Racheal assured her cousin. It almost seemed like she was trying to be *nice* until she said this: "I can hear you when you're not yelling perfectly fine."

"I don't know, do we just look in all of these rooms?" Nina suggested.

"If you want to stay here for 48 hours, then sure!" Racheal commented sarcastically. "There are too many rooms to count!"

"Not helping," Nina muttered to her daughter.

Suddenly, one of a million doors opened. Coming out of it was Angie White!!! The most AMAZING superstar in the WHOLE ENTIRE UNIVERSE (well, at least in Mo's opinion)!

Racheal wasn't surprised, she had seen her on social media, but she wasn't a fan of her music. Well, after all, she wasn't a fan of ANY music.

"Hello, may I help you with

anything?" Angie asked, her strong British accent showing.

Mo could barely breath! It was ANGIE WHITE for goodness sake!

"Oh...my...goodness!!!"Mo exclaimed.She was more excited than ever! Imagine meeting *your* favorite singer right after you got signed to a singing contract (well, a lot of them). It's literally the best feeling ever!

How do I know that? Those were the exact words Mo was

thinking in her mind.

"Oh, autographs?" asked Angie, walking over to them. "I can do that lickety-split and--"

"We're actually here to see an agent," Nina interrupted. "Mo over here just got signed as an artist."

"Oh, my gosh!" Angie squealed. "Welcome to the studio!" She shook Mo's hand.

Another door suddenly burst open. Coming out of it was the agent!

"Ah, I thought I had told the

secretary to tell visitors not to disturb the artists!" she groaned, walking to Angie and the Lemonts.

"No, no, they're not visitors," Angie explained, "I think they want to see YOU."

The agent looked up at Mo. "Mo Lemont!" She walked over to <u>her</u> and shook her hand. "It's nice to see you again. What is it that you need from me?"

"Well, I would like a little extension for

the contracts," said Mo. "Or

maybe you could take some of them back, whatever works for you."

"Oh, Mo, why didn't you just tell me in the first place?" she asked. "Of course I can make an extension! How does a *month* sound?" (She had just then realized that is a lot for a little kid.)

Mo sighed with relief. "Yes, thank you SO much!!"

"Oh, it's just great that you guys have found a solution!" Angie added. "Maybe I'll see you later?"

She was looking right at Mo.

"Sure," she croaked, watching Angieand

the agent walking down the long hall.

Mo had a great feeling in her chest. "Best day ever."

Chapter Seven: School

The Lemonts went out for frozen yogurt in celebration of Mo's excellence in singing. Right when they walked in the building, they saw a counter full of delicious and unique toppings. Mo ran over to the fresh, chocolate covered strawberries.

Those were her favorite. There were also many flavors, including strawberry: Mo's *favorite* FLAVOR.

"This is heaven!" she exclaimed, running over to the foam cups. "This place has *all* of my favorites!"

Georgia and Nina chuckled. It was cute to them how her face lit up because of a frozen delight. Moms!

Racheal refused to eat anything. I mean, how could she text, eat with a spoon, *and* insult Mo all at the same time? It just wouldn't work out.

Mo ended up getting strawberry yogurt with

choco-covered strawberries and sprinkles (as some of you know as *jimmies*).

Jared also got some fro-yo: of course, chocolate yogurt with chocolate sprinkles and mini chocolate brownies.

Those two were the only ones who ate, and they got in the car after they paid. "Are we going home now?" Racheal asked impatiently. "We've gone to like ten places already."

"Yes," Nina sighed.

They drove, and they drove

until they arrived at the Lemonts' house. When they parked in their driveway, Racheal unbuckled her seatbelt when she saw the house nearby and jumped out of the car right when they stopped.

Mo went inside carrying her trash and a grocery bag. She had to help because she was told to, but she would have helped anyways.

It was August eighteenth, and school would start in less than a month! Mo was ready to start at a new school, only having few great friends. She video chatted them every Saturday at four p.m. They all went to a school called Flora Elementary.

That school was kindergartenthrough eighth grade. Mo's new school in Alabama with Racheal in it :(was called L.K. (standing for Lionel King) Junior High. That school was grades five to nine. She would have gone to a middle school and then a high school if she was still in New York City, but it wasn't a big bummer if she just went to junior high.

On September first, it was the first day of school (it was ironic how they scheduled that).

Mo got out of bed at 6:30 a.m. that morning and took a shower. After that, she got all ready for school. Racheal got out of bed at 7:30 and ended up being tardy because class started at 8:00.

Mo was a little confused with the set up when she entered the school. There were three floors: the first for staff/unified arts, the second for 5-7 graders, and the third for 8-9. Why was there a whole floor for the teachers and art classes? They could have fit the music and art rooms on one of the other floors and put a good use to the extra floor. Well, their decision. Mo just ignored her puzzled brain and carried on with her new school.

When a girl realized Mo had a perplexed

look on her face, she walked over to her. "You new here?"

Mo nodded shyly.

"I'll show you around," she suggested. "My name's Savannah."

"Thanks!" Mo exclaimed. "My name's Mo."

"I know who you are," Savannah replied, beckoning her to the left of the hallway. "You played at my favorite restaurant.

Now which is your first class?"

"Mrs. Antonio," she answered. "Is your favorite

restaurant Rose Chip or Spaghetti Mountain?"

"Spaghetti Mountain," she explained. "Follow me."

Savannah lead Mo to a big classroom.

There were about six people in the room so far, and that showed she wasn't late, but she might have been a little early.

"Hello, you must be new!" a nice looking woman greeted. "Mo Lemont, I presume?"

"That's right!" she

answered confidently.

Being on stage made her confident around adults.

"My class is down the hall," Savannah whispered to her. "I gotta go."

Mo shot a thumbs up in her direction.

She smiled. New friends, nice teacher, Racheal all the way across the hall. She had a good feeling about L.K. Junior High. Until something made it even better, someone was sitting across the room.

That someone was Michael! Now THAT

was the best part of her day. She pulled her hair behind her ear while her cheeks were blushing.

"Oh, sup, Mo!" he exclaimed, smirking. "I didn't know you went to this school."

"Well, I--uh, this is my first day," Mo stuttered. "I moved here from New York and moved in with Racheal."

"Ooh, that must be hard," he replied, laughing.

"Ah, tell me about it!" Mo agreed.

They both laughed until the door busted open. That attracted everyone's attention.

"Speak of the devil," Mo muttered to Michael. He giggled.

Racheal looked up from her mini mirror and put away her eye shadow brush. That was the only thing that distracted her at school, for there were no phones allowed at school. She realized

Michael and Mo were getting ALONG. Like, ALONG, ALONG. She hated that! With everyone staring at her, she stomped out of the room madly.

"Okay..." Mrs. Antonio said, confused.

"Apparently whatever she had to say wasn't that important."

The class laughed.

Racheal stomped down the hall madly.

"Ugh!" she thought. "Why

does Mo get MY MAN?! I HAVE to do something about it...and I know the EXACT place..."

Chapter Eight:
NO GO FOR MO!

Mo's next class was math in Mr. Snink's class. She thought that was an unusual name: it reminded her of her best friend Cassidy. She loved snakes *and* pink! Snink!

"We are going to start with reviewing decimals, so you can start remembering them from last year," he explained in a kind voice to the class. "So, unpack your stuff and sit down at any desk you would like."

Mo chose to sit next to a nice-looking girl with amber eyes and black hair.

"Mr. Snink is SO nice," she remarked.

"Yeah, he is," Mo agreed. "I'm Mo."

"Nice to meet you," the girl replied. "I'm Tabitha. You can call me Tabby."

Mo was smiling cheek to cheek. Three awesome friends plus two awesome takes equals five amazing highlights to her school!

"So, let's go over place value," Mr. Snink told the class.

The class listened to their teacher until they had to work in their math books.

When the school day was over, Mo and Racheal got picked up by Georgia and Nina. She had a big singing gig at Operation Hamburger. It was at 6:30, So she got a dinner break there.

"I am so excited!" Mo exclaimed, ignoring

Racheal's dirty looks. "Me, too!" Nina agreed.

Georgia silently texted her friends, just like Racheal.

3 hours later, they were off to Operation Hamburger. Mo practiced the song she would sing later, while Racheal plugged her ears.

They arrived in about fifteen minutes. Mo got on stage and sang her best song yet: The Ocean, Sea and River. Or for short, Water.

She started singing it, when a cold shiver trickled her

spine. As she realized it was water dropping on her head, she knew immediately knew who did it. Racheal! She did it out of jealously to ruin her performance! How rude!

"What?" Racheal *innocently* asked from above the stage with an empty bucket in her hands. "You said the song was called Water, so I wanted to make the performance INTERESTING."

Mo just kept singing, when something strange happened. Racheal started shouting, "NO GO FOR MO! NO GO FOR MO!"

just like in her dream!

When she chanted it about six times, people started chanting, "Go, go, Mo! Go, go, Mo!"

Mo was worried they would follow in Racheal's footsteps, but apparently, they heard wrong! <u>They</u> thought she was saying, "Go, go, Mo!" Mo felt good that they were mistaken. So, Mo just kept singing.

When Racheal finally came down from the platform with a railing above the stage, Nina kissed her head and said,

"That was a very nice thing to do, chanting 'Go, go Mo!' You've finally gone through that hatred faze!"

Racheal replied by rolling her eyes and going back to texting on her phone.

When the performance was done, and the dinner was eaten, they all went home and relaxed. Mo watched some television. Racheal checked her social media again.

Nina and Georgia talked about Mom stuff Jared watched football. They all did their own thing. Just like always.

"What a day!" Mo thought as she got in bed.

It was an overwhelming day: first day of school, first record of friends met in a day, first soaking wet performance! Wow!

It was a long day for Mo, and she had no idea that the next day would be even more crazier.

Chapter Nine: Lights Out

Mo woke up bright and early again and got ready. Nina had a feeling Racheal would have a tardy streak when she was late again.

Mrs. Antonio and Mr. Snink were great again, and so were Mo's three friends. Mo was really loving decimals, especially because of the fun way Mr. S was teaching it. Racheal's jealousy grew and grew as she watched Mo and her group of friends at lunch and recess. When Michael laughed at one of Mo's jokes, her hand became a fist. She would get back at her for making her look...*nice* in Operation Hamburger. And she was planning on succeeding this time. Just like an evil villain against a powerful superhero. The superhero usually wins...but not this time (more on that later).

Mo's day started to get crazy when it was 10:00. She had a loud assembly, and right after a quick lunch and recess. Then onto a crazy outdoor science experiment. But the craziness didn't stop there! In music, Mo had to plug her ears watching band practice. After that, her bus swerved violently because of a squirrel! She went right to a gig, and this is where the *real* drama starts.

Her performance was at Rose Chip once again because the owner loved her singing. Everything was going great for the first three minutes, but then suddenly the power went out!

"Come on, Racheal!" Mo muttered to herself.

Yeah, I agree. She could have gone better than that. And she went with the classic power drainer. Wait a second, I'm on Mo's side! Ignore that, back to the story.

Gasps shot out all over the room. A baby screamed. A child laughed. A girl groaned. That girl was Mo.

"I guess I'll just keep singing," Mo thought.

She softly continued her song, but when people started singing with her, she got louder.

Mo was almost startled when a phone's light flashed across the room. Mo felt happy. Light was around. Figuratively and literally. No matter what Racheal did, she couldn't shut off the light in Mo's heart.

Good times and bad, the light would be there forever.

Chapter Ten:

Hanging out with Racheal

After that crazy day, Mo fell asleep right away. Everything seemed so rushed, she was out like a light! Ha, get it?

It was hard to get up that morning because of the fact that Mo couldn't sleep that night. Racheal's phone kept going off. And the worst part is that the volume was maximum level. Again. Come on, Racheal!

"Ugh, Mom, I don't want to get up!" Mo groaned, her face dug into her pillow.

This is the way Racheal acted *every* morning. She eventually woke up and rushed to get ready.

In grammar, Mo was learning about similes. She came up with "His tears rolled down his cheeks like rain on a window."

"Great job, Mo!" the teacher exclaimed, impressed with her student's use of personification.

After grammar was lunch. Michael, Savannah, Tabby, and Mo were talking about a show that was recently cancelled when someone suddenly sat at the edge of the table right next to Michael. It was Racheal.

It was *always* Racheal.

"Hey, guys," she said, looking dreamily at Michael.

"Hello, Racheal," Mo greeted through her clenched teeth. Her nose twitched as she tried to sound nice. It was hard. "What are you, uh, doing here?"

"I just wanted to say hi

to my dear cousin Mich--
I mean Mo," she replied,
still staring at Michael
dreamily.

"Hey, does anyone else
have to go to the
bathroom?" Michael
asked, creeped out by
Racheal's expression.

Savannah, Tabby, and
Mo all nodded, following
Michael to the bathroom
area. Racheal trailed
behind them. The girls
went into the girls'

bathroom and Michael in the boys'.

As the girls each entered a stall, Racheal started talking. "Girls, I need to tell you something."

"No, Racheal, you know it's awkward talking while going to the bathroom," Mo argued.

Racheal just kept talking. "I want you to back off!

"What?" Savannah asked. "Back off what?"

"Michael, duh!" Tabby answered.

"We can be friends with him if we want to," Mo argued. "We can hang out with him if we want to. So *you* back off."

Mo knew Racheal was rolling her eyes even if she couldn't see her.

"Exactly," Racheal said. "If you can hang out with

him, so can I!"

"Please tell me Racheal's *not* going to

hang out with us all of the time," Savannah whispered to Mo as they left the bathroom.

"It's either that or no Michael," Mo sighed.

"Or..." Tabby interrupted. "I have a plan..."

"You sound like my Aunt Nina," Mo realized.

"What is it?" Savannah questioned. "Is it effective?"

"Most definitely," she replied with an evil look on her face. Now *she* was acting like a villain.

"Tell us!" Mo shouted impatiently.

"Tell you what?" Racheal asked. "If I'm going to be part of this group, I might as well be part of the conversations you have."

"Oh, nothing," Savannah told her. "Just something about sixth grade. Nothing you would understand."

"You know I was in sixth grade last year, right?" she said to her.

"Yeah, umm...I have to go get something from the classroom," Tabby suddenly *remembered*.

"Oh, yeah, me too,"

Michaelagreed,coming out of theboy's bathroom.

"We'll come with you," Mo croaked, putting her arm around Savannah's shoulder.

"Oh, yeah--" Racheal started to say,when

she got cut off.

"Racheal, why are you hanging out with a bunch of sixth graders?" one of her texters interrupted.

"Come over to the popular table!"

"But--" Racheal replied. She looked at Michael and her texter. "Fine. I'll be right there."

When she left, Racheal turned around to the girls, her evil villain sense kicking on. "I'll be back!" Michael tried not to laugh but busted into giggles when she left the room.

The four of them

rushed to their classroom. Luckily, the teacher wasn't there!

And Mo didn't feel like lying. Not after what just had happened.

"Okay, what's your plan?" Mo asked Tabby.

"Ooh, there's a plan!" Michael exclaimed.

"Come on, just tell us!" Savannah whined impatiently.

"Okay, okay, here's the

plan: we should pretend to suddenly not be friends anymore because of a *fight*," she explained, "and when Racheal tries to hang out with Michael, he acts super snobby. Racheal wouldn't want to hang out with him anymore, and everything can go back to normal again!"

"Perfect!" Michael agreed. "I'm all up for being snobby at Racheal." "It could work," Mo said.

"Yeah, it could," Savannah added. "And perfectly!"

"Okay, when do we start?" Michael asked.

"Tomorrow at recess," Tabby answered. "We'll *fight* right in front of Racheal!"

The four of them cheered excitedly. They went back down to the cafeteria and talked with Racheal staring at them from the "popular table".

They secretly talked about their awesome plan at recess. Would it work? They didn't know. They would just have to find out the next day.

Chapter Eleven:

Trying the Plan

The next day came slowly for Mo, Savannah, Tabby, and Michael. They were greatly anticipating their next recess. The plan Tabby had made was fantastic, and they had all practiced acting mad at each other after school.

They practiced their stomps, they practiced their fists, they practiced their mad expressions. They were ready.

The four all sat together at lunch just like any old day, but recess was not just like any old day. It was a new day.

Their plan was that Mo would accidentally trip Michael and he would get mad at her. Then that would cause Savannah and Tabby to split up from them because of their fighting. Mo and Michael would go separate ways, then they would have to wait for the magic to happen: Racheal hanging out with Michael.

They did exactly that at recess, and after the "explosion of friendship" happened, Michael went on the opposite side of the playground than Mo.

He sat alone on a tree stump until Racheal came over to him.

"What are you doing?" she asked, making sure her hair was as perfectly perfect as it always was. She tried to sound sad but her words couldn't help sounding happy. "Did you get in a fight with my cousin and your...friends?"

"Yeah," answered Michael, his acting on

fleek. "It's really upsetting."

"I could hang out with you," Racheal suggested quickly.

"Fine," Michael retorted rudely.

This plan was going well! Racheal was falling for it!

"Umm...okay," she replied, a little confused with his unusual behavior. She just guessed it was a rough fight and he was upset. "What do you wanna do?"

"Nothing!" Michael whined childishly. If this wasn't acting, NO ONE would want to hang out with him instead of everyone.

"Oh. Well, I'll see you later then," Racheal replied. She walked away, realizing Michael isn't the kind of person she wanted to go I mean, hang out with.

"That was quick," Savannah observed happily.

"Now she can leave us alone!" Mo added, walking over to her and Tabby. "Let's go over to Michael."

"Go away," he complained, joking around.

Mo had a confused

look on her face, but when Michael's pout faded away and he laughed, she was relieved.

Mo went home that day feeling happy.

Sure, she still had Racheal, but she had a lot of other things, too. Family, friends, an awesome town. She was getting used to her home. And she had a feeling that it would be like that for a long time. As long as she kept staying Mo Lemont.

This book was written and designed by Claire

Burbank

Mo Lemont: Hoefler
Text, Jazz LET, Helvetica
Neue

68127529R00087

Made in the USA
Middletown, DE
28 March 2018